Green Thumbs, Everyone

OTHER YEARLING BOOKS ABOUT THE POLK STREET KIDS YOU WILL ENJOY:

THE BEAST IN MS. ROONEY'S ROOM
FISH FACE
THE CANDY CORN CONTEST
DECEMBER SECRETS
IN THE DINOSAUR'S PAW
THE VALENTINE STAR
LAZY LIONS, LUCKY LAMBS
SNAGGLE DOODLES
PURPLE CLIMBING DAYS
SAY "CHEESE"
SUNNY-SIDE UP
PICKLE PUSS
BEAST AND THE HALLOWEEN HORROR
EMILY ARROW PROMISES TO DO BETTER THIS YEAR
MONSTER RABBIT RUNS AMUCK!
WAKE UP, EMILY, IT'S MOTHER'S DAY

Plus the Polk Street Specials

WRITE UP A STORM WITH THE POLK STREET SCHOOL
COUNT YOUR MONEY WITH THE POLK STREET SCHOOL
TURKEY TROUBLE
THE POSTCARD PEST
SHOW TIME AT THE POLK STREET SCHOOL
LOOK OUT, WASHINGTON, D.C.!

YEARLING BOOKS are designed especially to entertain and enlighten young people. Patricia Reilly Giff, consultant to this series, received her bachelor's degree from Marymount College and a master's degree in history from St. John's University. She holds a Professional Diploma in reading and a Doctorate of Humane Letters from Hofstra University. She was a teacher and reading consultant for many years, and is the author of numerous books for young readers.

For a complete listing of all Yearling titles, write to
Dell Readers Service, P.O. Box 1045,
South Holland, IL 60473.

A POLK STREET SPECIAL

Green Thumbs, Everyone

• • • •

Patricia Reilly Giff

Illustrated by Blanche Sims

A Yearling Book

Published by
Bantam Doubleday Dell Books for Young Readers
a division of
Bantam Doubleday Dell Publishing Group, Inc.
1540 Broadway
New York, New York 10036

ISBN: 0-440-41134-3

Printed in the United States of America
March 1996
10 9 8 7 6 5 4 3 2 1
CWO

For Bob Bullington,
who loved gardens

Chapter 1

It was Monday night, after supper. Richard Best bumped his bike over a crack in the sidewalk.

Head down, he raced along.

It felt as if he were going fifty miles an hour. Maybe a hundred.

Too bad he couldn't cross the street for

another four days. Not unless it was an emergency.

All he could do was go around the block.

It was the boringest ride in the world.

And all because of Holly, his tattletale sister. She had caught him riding on Linden Avenue the other day.

She had told their mother.

Of course.

"Cars whizzing around all over the place," Holly had said, tossing her head. "And there was my brother, Beast, on his bike. He was one inch from being a road pizza."

Holly had put her hand on her chest. "My heart almost stopped," she had told their mother.

Right now, Beast circled the block for the third time.

He thought about Holly.

Holly the pest.

Holly's heart almost stopped about forty times a day.

Beast watched the sidewalk rushing by beneath him.

As soon as he got out of punishment, he was going to ride over to the Stone Street Park.

There was a stream with frogs, and little silver fish, and snails . . .

Holly never went near Stone Street Park.

He could do anything he wanted . . . drive his bike right over the bridge, no hands, or go fishing in the stream.

Beast could see a bike coming around the corner.

It was coming straight toward him.

He could see legs too. They were pedaling up and down as fast as they could.

Beast tried to keep his head down. He had to watch for big cracks in the sidewalk.

There were a million of them.

He'd gotten one bloody knee this week already.

But the other bike didn't stop.

It didn't even try to make room for him.

Beast jammed his feet on the brakes.

He was swerving.

He knew he was going to fall.

He hoped he wasn't going to fall on the knee with the scab.

He was sliding over . . . sliding fast.

Then he was on the ground.

The other bike was on top of him. A black one with neon stripes.

And so was Drake Evans, the meanest kid in the whole Polk Street School.

Beast inched his way out from underneath.

He blinked a couple of times.

He would never let Drake Evans know he was crying.

"Big baby," Drake said.

Drake grabbed his black-and-neon bike. He pulled it up with two fingers.

Drake was the strongest kid in the Polk Street School too.

"Stay off this side of the block," Drake told him.

Beast tried to pull his own bike up with two fingers.

He couldn't.

The bike dropped on his toe.

He wanted to scream.

He jumped up and down.

He stopped as fast as he could, though.

Drake was laughing all over the place.

Beast stared at him . . . a mean Rex Robot stare.

He had gotten three Rex Robots for his birthday.

They were all mean, all tough.

He dragged his bike down the block.

He could see that Drake Evans's knee was bleeding.

Too bad for Drake Evans.

Too bad for him too.

His own knee was bleeding again.

And his pinky toe was probably crushed.

Worse yet, he couldn't even take his bike around the block anymore.

Chapter 2

It was after school on Tuesday. Beast marched down the street and around the corner.

So what about Drake Evans?

Beast still had three more days to stay on his own block.

He had to do something.

If Drake came one step toward him, he'd race around the block to his own house.

He had left the screen door open a crack.

Beast blasted the trees, the telephone pole, and Mrs. Elliot's dog, Lester, with his Rex Robot gun.

He blasted Drake Evans's house, and Drake's driveway, and the black-and-neon bike.

Good thing Drake couldn't see him.

Emily Arrow was standing on the corner.

He'd blast her next.

He lifted the ray gun.

Emily spotted him. "No you don't!" she yelled.

Emily raced down the street away from him.

Mrs. Elliot's dog, Lester, raced after her.

Beast started to laugh.

Mrs. Elliot wasn't laughing, though.

She stuck her head out the door. "Get back here, Lester!" she shouted.

"Don't worry," Beast called. "I'll get him."

He charged around the corner.

Lester was gone.

So was Emily.

"I see you," he yelled to Emily.

He didn't see her.

He didn't see Lester either. And Lester was hard to miss.

Lester was skinny and tall. He always looked as if he had a cold. His eyes were droopy and his nose was wet.

Beast stood without moving a muscle.

He couldn't hear either one of them.

He could hear Mrs. Elliot, though. "Lesssss-ter!" she was screaming.

"Maybe in one of the backyards," Beast said.

He walked up Mr. Meno's driveway. "I know where you are," he told Emily.

He blasted Mr. Meno's garbage cans with the Rex Robot gun.

He walked back down the driveway.

There wasn't even a bush big enough to hide behind.

He could hear Emily laughing, though.

Beast stood on tiptoe to look over the fence between the yards.

There she was . . . and Lester too.

She must have climbed over the top. Lester must have dug under the bottom.

There was a pile of new dirt where Beast was standing.

Lester and Emily were crouched down behind a huge snowball bush.

Beast put his feet into a hole in the wooden fence.

He started to climb.

He could hear the wood cracking.

Emily spotted him. She began to make faces and wave her arms. "Don't . . . ," she began.

Beast grinned. She couldn't get away.

She was stuck in the corner of the yard, pointing at something.

He wondered why she looked so wet.

Beast got to the top of the fence.

He dropped over the other side . . . right into a spray of water.

"Yeow!" he yelled.

It was a sprinkler, going around in a circle.

Mrs. Alonzo's sprinkler.

He couldn't believe it.

He was in Mrs. Alonzo's yard . . . and so were Emily and Lester.

Mrs. Alonzo was the toughest woman in the world.

Tougher than the sixth-grade teacher at the Polk Street School.

Splat.

The sprinkler hit him again.

In one second Beast was soaked. Water was everywhere. It had plastered down his hair and his T-shirt.

His sneakers were filled with it.

He stepped out of the way, into a bunch of stuff . . . flowers maybe, or vegetables.

Mrs. Alonzo was always working on her garden.

Beast took another step.

He landed on a plant that looked like a fat cabbage.

Emily was staring at him.

Her eyes were open wide.

So was her mouth.

Water was streaming from the ends of her ponytails.

Lester looked as if he had just taken a bath.

Just then Beast heard something.

Bang.

Mrs. Alonzo's kitchen door.

Emily and Lester were crouched down low.

They looked as if they were disappearing into the ground.

Beast reached for the top of the fence with both hands.

"Who's that?" Mrs. Alonzo screeched. "Who's in my garden?"

From where he was, Beast could just about hear Mrs. Elliot's voice. "Lesssster!"

He could hear Mrs. Alonzo coming closer . . . much closer.

He took his hands off the fence.

He raced across the yard, his feet squishing.

CABBAGE

"Stop!" Mrs. Alonzo was yelling.

He hopped across a row of spiky-looking plants with tassels, and down the driveway.

He started down the street.

He could see Drake Evans in his driveway.

Quickly Beast turned his head away.

He started to walk like Rex Robot.

Head up.

Shoulders back.

He could feel his sneakers squishing, and something else . . . a stone under his crushed pinky toe.

He tried not to limp.

He kept going until he reached Linden Avenue.

Chapter 3

It was after supper that night.

Beast was in his garage. He was building a satellite station.

Holly was in the garage too. "He's building garbage," she told her friend Joanne.

Beast started to whistle.

It was more like a loud whisper than a whistle.

He still couldn't get it exactly right.

It was sounding better every day, though.

Besides, he was drowning Holly out.

She had to scream to make Joanne hear her. "Don't worry!" she was yelling. "We're going to get that reward!"

Beast stopped whistling as soon as Holly walked her bike out of the garage.

His cheeks hurt, and his lips.

He leaned forward and heard Joanne say, "All we have to do is go back to the scene of the crime. We can measure the footprints."

"Right," Holly said. "We'll check out the evidence and . . ."

Beast stepped out of the garage. "What reward?"

Too late.

Holly slammed the garage door down.

She missed his satellite station by a thread.

Beast walked around in front of her.

She had thrown one leg over her bike.

Joanne was holding up her own bike, kicking the tires.

It looked as if they'd be flat any minute.

Too bad for big-mouth Joanne.

"Out of my way," Holly told him.

She coasted around him and down the driveway.

Beast looked after them, thinking about a reward.

He wondered what kind of reward.

Money?

He and Emily didn't have one cent saved for the summer.

They could use a reward too.

He opened the garage door again.

His bike was lying on its side in the back.

He marched over to it.

He tried to pick it up with three fingers.

It crashed on his toes.

He yanked it up, thinking about Holly and Joanne. Suppose they crossed the street?

His mother and father might not mind if he crossed too.

Not if they knew he was going to get a pile of money . . . and buy them something nice.

Maybe a new car for his father. One of those sport things that had spokes in the tires.

Beast pedaled down the driveway.

Holly and Joanne were turning the corner.

They didn't cross the street.

Excellent.

He sped after them.

They never looked back.

They were so dumb.

They barely even looked in front of them, they were so busy talking.

He snorted. They'd never win that reward. He'd get ahead of them and . . .

He thought about his mother.

What could he get for her?

Maybe a whole new kitchen.

She was always complaining that the stove was a hundred years old. And the refrigerator didn't make good ice cubes. The toaster was the worst, she said.

He'd throw in a toaster too.

He hit a big crack in the sidewalk.

He zigzagged past a couple of garbage cans into Mr. Meno's driveway. He crashed into Mr. Meno's parked car.

He stood up. His knee was bleeding again. He could see a scratch on the side of the car.

Good thing it was an old car.

Probably as old as his mother's stove.

Mr. Meno might not notice one little scratch across the door.

Beast stuck his finger in his mouth and wet it. Then he ran it across the scratch.

It wasn't so little.

How could he have done that?

He felt his heart begin to pound.

He looked up.

Two doors down, Drake Evans was standing at his window.

Beast ducked his head. He pushed his bike backward as fast as he could.

He didn't stop until he got to his own driveway.

Chapter 4

Beast zoomed up the driveway.

He drove his bike straight to the garage.

He jumped off at the last second.

The bike kept going.

Right into the corner where it belonged.

He could hear Holly talking to Joanne on the back step.

They were back, then.

He took a step toward them.

It was almost dark. He'd sneak up like lightning.

They'd never hear him.

He tiptoed around the side of the garage.

Holly had ears like a fox. "Do you have to drive the bike into the garage like that every time?" she asked.

"He's just like my brother," said Joanne. "Doesn't care about one thing."

"And he leaves the screen door open," Holly said. "Bugs flying in and out like crazy."

Beast stepped out of the shadows. "What's the reward?"

"You don't have to know everything," Holly said.

Just then the kitchen light went on. "Do you know what time it is, Richard?" Beast's mother said. "You still have school for a few days. You have to take a bath and finish your homework."

Beast stamped across the yard. He stepped over Holly and Joanne and went into the house.

"You should make Holly come in too," he said. "She looks as if she needs a bath worse than I do."

"Mind your own business!" Holly screamed at the top of her lungs.

Beast's mother frowned. "Don't run the water to the top of the tub, and don't leave your clothes . . ."

Beast didn't wait to hear the rest.

He took the steps two at a time up to the bathroom.

Actually he liked taking a bath.

He'd pile the water in and have a war with about fifteen Rex Robots.

He turned the water on full blast.

He rolled up his pants and left his shirt on.

The bath didn't get really warm until it was filled to the top.

Beast stood in the tub. He put a Rex Robot on the windowsill and dived him into the water.

Beast took a quick look outside. Holly and Joanne were still sitting on the steps, right beneath him.

"Mrs. Alonzo said she wouldn't put up reward signs yet," Holly said.

For a moment Beast stood still. He felt as if he couldn't move.

Mrs. Alonzo. He couldn't believe it.

"This will be easy," Holly said.

"We know it was a kid . . . ," Joanne began.

"A couple of kids," Holly said. "Teenagers."

"But why would they want to ruin her garden?" Joanne said.

"Mean," said Holly. "Criminals."

For a minute everything was quiet.

Then Holly said, "I don't care about the reward. It will just be good to see them taken off to jail. Poor old lady loves her garden."

"Yeah," said Joanne.

Beast slid back into the tub.

He didn't even care that his clothes were soaked.

They were talking about Mrs. Alonzo's garden, and about Lester and Emily and him.

Lester was lucky he was a dog.

They'd never put a dog in jail.

But what about Emily?

Beast sank down in the tub.

And what about him?

Chapter 5

On Wednesday there was a substitute teacher. It was long, skinny Mrs. Barrow.

She raced them through attendance, through milk money, through reading.

Beast ducked his head when she told them to pass in their homework.

Last night he had never gotten to his.

He'd do it at lunchtime today as fast as he could.

Right now he was bursting to talk to Emily.

Every time he tried, Mrs. Barrow tapped the desk with her pencil. "No time to waste," she said.

Beast pulled out his notebook quietly.

As quietly as Rex Robot.

He didn't even have a pencil that worked.

He took chunks off the top with his teeth, until he could see a little lead poking up.

Then he ducked behind Matthew Jackson so he could write.

E.

We are in the werst truble.

Mrs. Alonzo has a reward.

For us.
For the gardn stamping.
Singed,
Richard Best

Suddenly he realized. The whole class was quiet.

Too quiet.

No one was moving or coughing.

No one was even breathing.

And someone was standing right in front of him.

Mrs. Barrow.

"Are you writing notes to Emily?" she asked.

Emily looked up. "I don't think so."

Beast nodded. "Yes."

Mrs. Barrow sighed. "We have no time to waste."

"I know." Beast crumpled up the note. He shoved it inside his desk.

"Besides," said Mrs. Barrow, "it's time for recess."

"Yahoodie!" yelled Matthew.

Beast wanted to yell "yahoodie" too.

He didn't, though.

Mrs. Barrow was still standing in front of him, her whole face crinkled up like a prune.

She clapped her hands. "Line up at the side of the door."

Beast raced for the line.

Emily raced after him. "How come you're sending me a note?" she asked.

Beast looked over his shoulder.

Was Mrs. Barrow going to stare at him for the rest of his life?

"I'll tell you outside," he told Emily.

"Yahoodie," she said.

The class marched down the hall.

They stopped to look at the fourth-grade bulletin board.

The class had done pictures of vegetables and flowers.

Beast looked at drawings of a pile of lima beans and droopy yellow daisies.

ALL THIS FROM SEEDS, it said on top.

"Disgusting," Matthew said.

"Half dead," said Beast.

"Lovely work," said Mrs. Barrow.

They headed for the back door and out into the schoolyard.

It was a great day. The sun looked like a fat orange.

"Don't look at the sun," Matthew said. "You can get blind in about ten years from it."

"Don't worry," Beast said. "I won't."

He looked around for Emily.

She was heading for the hopscotch game.

"Hey!" he yelled, and ran to catch up with her.

"Are you really sending me notes?" she asked.

"We're going to be in jail any minute," he said. "The police are looking for us. There's even a reward."

Emily glanced around. She looked worried. "They're not after me," she said.

"Mrs. Alonzo," he said without moving his lips.

He looked up at the school windows.

He could see Drake Evans sharpening his pencil.

Drake Evans was watching him. He probably knew everything . . . the garden . . . the car.

Maybe Drake would call the police.

Then Beast saw that Emily was staring at him.

She had round red spots on each cheek.

"What can we do?" she said.

Beast sighed.

Emily was luckier than he was.

Suppose Mr. Meno found out that he was the one who had scratched up the car?

Chapter 6

"Come on," Emily whispered after school on Wednesday. She was tiptoeing down the street.

Emily was the greatest tiptoer in the world.

Beast swallowed.

They might get caught anyway.

Emily's head was down. Her back was hunched over.

Beast hunched his back over too.

He stared down at the ground.

He watched the dirt, and the pebbles, and the weeds.

The sun was hot on the back of his neck.

They were almost to Mrs. Alonzo's house.

Emily had told him, "We have to take a look at that garden. We have to see how bad it is."

"Plenty bad," he had said.

Holly had told their mother and father over breakfast. "It looks as if an animal chewed the whole place up," she had said between bites of Wheat Chex. "It's horrible."

Beast's mother had shaken her head. "Sad."

"Yes," Beast had said.

"What do you know?" Holly had said back.

"I'm probably going to get the reward," he had told her, "and you've got Wheat Chex all over your big mouth."

Holly had kicked his leg under the table, kicked it where there wasn't one inch of skin.

His luck to have been stuck with a sister who was the toughest kid in the world.

Right now he stopped sneaking along the path behind Mrs. Alonzo's fence. He gave his shin a rub.

He probably had a black-and-blue mark as big as a baseball.

He could hear noises behind him.

Scrabbling sounds on the pebbles.

He bet it was Holly, chasing him, trying to get the reward for herself.

Too bad for Holly.

He'd get the reward and he wouldn't give her one cent. Not one . . .

What was he thinking of?

He couldn't get that reward.

No one could.

He sneaked a quick look over his shoulder.

It was Lester, Mrs. Elliot's dog.

Lester, who had probably messed the garden worse than he and Emily had.

Lester, who had dug himself right under Mrs. Alonzo's fence.

Lester, who had dug his paws right into the middle of everything.

"Go home, Lester," Beast whispered. He put his feet in a hole in the fence.

Next to him, Emily was boosting herself up.

Lester was panting all over the place.

He grabbed a piece of Beast's jeans.

"Get out of here, Lester," Beast said. "No playing."

Emily looked over her shoulder and frowned. "Everyone is going to hear."

Lester reached for a bigger piece of Beast's jeans.

He took a chunk of skin with it.

The same little chunk that Holly had kicked before.

"Yeow!" Beast yelled.

Mrs. Alonzo's screen door banged open.

Emily and Beast dived off the fence.

They could hear Mrs. Alonzo.

They couldn't see her, though.

Lester had dived on top of them.

He was heavy as lead.

Beast raised his head a little to see.

Mrs. Alonzo was talking to herself . . . or maybe to one of her plants. "You poor

thing," she said. "You poor, poor thing. If I had more energy, I'd . . ." She stopped to push a strand of hair out of her eye.

She didn't look as tough as usual. She looked a little sad.

Lester was licking the back of Beast's neck.

Beast couldn't even raise his hand to stop him.

Mrs. Alonzo was about two inches away.

If she even looked up . . .

She didn't, though.

She kept talking and snipping little dead leaves off her plants.

Beast could feel his T-shirt getting wetter and wetter.

Next to him, Emily's face was buried in the pebbles.

Finally Mrs. Alonzo went back into her house.

They waited a minute.

Then Emily sat up. "Why do you let that dog lie all over you, slobbering like that?"

Beast gave Lester a little push.

Lester slid off. He began to tug on Beast's sneakers.

Then Beast and Emily moved a little closer to the garden.

It was a mess.

Footprints. Plants trampled. Chunks of grass torn up.

Emily looked sad. She looked worried. "We're in terrible trouble," she said.

"I know it," Beast said.

"But I think I know what we could do," Emily said.

Chapter 7

That night Beast couldn't get to sleep.

Everything was hot . . . his bedroom, the sheets, the pillow.

He could hear his mother and father talking in their bedroom.

First the rumble of his father's voice.

Then his mother's. Lighter. She was laughing about something.

His mother had a nice laugh.

Beast pulled the pillow around to find a cooler spot.

It was a good thing his mother and father didn't know about him . . . about the things he had done this week.

How terrible if they found out there was a reward for him, just like a criminal on TV.

And suppose she found out about Mr. Meno's scratched-up car?

And the other thing. Going off the block this afternoon when he still had two more days to go.

"It's an emergency," Emily had told him. "You have to come to my house. I have to show you how we can fix this business with Mrs. Alonzo."

Beast sat up in bed.

His feet felt hot, and his hands too.

Maybe if he had a glass of water, a glass of water with an ice cube.

He could just see the ice cube floating around, cold as an igloo.

He listened. His mother and father had stopped talking.

Everything was quiet.

He slid out of bed.

He had to get a drink of water.

He stopped to look out the window. He thought about being in trouble.

"Don't worry," Emily had said. "We're going to fix everything right up."

Beast opened his bedroom door.

He didn't see how they were going to fix everything up.

"See?" Emily had kept saying as she pointed. "See?"

All he had seen was a space in back of her

garage . . . a weedy old spot with empty soda cans and junk piled up.

He went down the stairs.

It was dark in the hallway, so dark he couldn't see one thing.

Suddenly he thought of Drake Evans.

Drake Evans always saw everything that was going on.

He probably knew all about Mr. Meno's car.

He probably knew about Mrs. Alonzo's garden.

And he probably knew about Beast's going off the block.

Drake Evans was going to get the reward . . . and he was going to tell about everything else.

That's the kind of kid Drake Evans was.

Even though it was hot in the living room, maybe ninety degrees, Beast shivered.

He went through the dining room and headed for the kitchen.

He sighed. If only he could go back a couple of days.

He'd do everything differently.

He bumped into the edge of the kitchen table . . . right into the corner.

Oof.

Then someone screamed . . . screamed loud enough to wake everyone.

And a minute later Holly was telling their mother and father, "My heart almost stopped. I thought he was a criminal."

"I just wanted to get—" he kept trying to say.

"Sneaking around," Holly kept saying. "Stopping my heart. Why does he have to do these things?"

Beast's mother was shaking her head as if she didn't know.

"I was just—" Beast began again.

"A person can't even get a drink on a hot night," Holly said.

Beast's father was frowning. "I think we'd better get back to bed," he said.

He looked at Beast. ". . . And stay there."

Chapter 8

Beast stood at the corner on Thursday after school. He watched a car go by, and then another.

"Emergency," he told himself. It was definitely an emergency.

He could hear someone breathing behind him. Someone with a cold?

He spun around. It was Lester.

"Go home, will you?" Beast said.

The dog didn't move.

Beast picked up a stick. He threw it down the street. "Go get it."

Lester sat and watched him.

Someone else was watching too.

Beast looked over his shoulder slowly.

Drake Evans was sitting on his front steps, eyes squinched together, staring at Beast.

Drake knew Beast was crossing the street.

So what?

Just let Drake tell.

Beast would . . . He sighed. There was nothing he could do.

He stepped off the curb.

A car horn blared.

He jumped back.

He looked over his shoulder. Drake was still staring.

Beast made believe he didn't notice.

This time he looked carefully before he sped across the street.

He could hear Lester padding along behind him all the way to Emily's house on Stone Street.

Emily was behind her garage.

She looked hot. She looked tired.

She looked angry.

"I've been working at this all by myself," she said.

Beast looked at the garden Emily had started.

It wasn't a garden yet.

It was still a raggedy mess.

All the soda cans were gone, though, and so were some of the weeds.

Emily nodded at him. "There's another rake in the garage."

She looked at Lester. "Put one foot in

this garden," she said, "and you're dog food."

Beast began to rake. Little rake lines appeared in the packed dirt.

It was hard work. The hardest he had ever done. The soil was hard as a rock, and there were about a million weeds.

He looked across at Emily. Her bangs were stuck to her forehead. "If we can just get this ready to plant today," she began. "Get rid of these few weeds . . ."

They'd never do it in a million years.

He kept raking, though.

They were going to plant everything . . . lettuce, and carrots, and radishes, and a whole bunch of flowers. Then they were going to give all of it to Mrs. Alonzo.

Mrs. Alonzo would love it.

Emily knew what he was thinking. She

brushed at her bangs. "It'll be worth all this work," she said.

Beast nodded. He was getting sunburned. Blisters were popping out on his fingers.

The earth was getting softer.

The weeds were getting fewer.

Beast began to think maybe he'd be a farmer when he grew up.

He felt as if someone was watching.

He looked up quickly.

No one was at the fence, or in the driveway. Still, he felt as if someone was there.

Lester felt it too. His head was on one side and his tail was wagging slowly.

Then they heard someone calling. It was Emily's mother. "Dinner," she said.

Beast looked at all they had done.

Emily was right.

They'd be able to plant tomorrow.

If only everything grew before Mrs.

Alonzo found out who had ruined her garden.

He started home. His mother would have dinner ready too.

But all the way home, he still kept thinking about someone watching.

He hoped it wasn't someone who was trying to get the reward.

Chapter 9

It was Friday. A great day.

School had been over for two weeks.

Beast's punishment was over.

And one of these days, as soon as the garden was finished, he was going to stay on the block for another week.

Without telling anyone.

To make up for all the emergencies.

The best thing of all was the garden.

Little spikes of green were coming up all over the place.

A row of radishes that zigzagged along next to the garage.

Marigold leaves.

Some other plants near the fence. He forgot what they were called.

And no one had talked about the reward in a couple of days.

Maybe Holly had forgotten all about it.

And Drake.

Beast was still worried, though, worried about Mr. Meno's car.

Last night he had seen Mr. Meno outside. He had been washing the car.

Beast hadn't stopped to look for more than a moment.

Was Mr. Meno bending over?

Was he looking at the long scratch on the door?

Beast started down his path.

Mr. Meno would be at work right now.

He always took an early train.

Beast could go over to Mr. Meno's driveway.

He could take another quick look at the car.

Maybe the scratch was gone.

Maybe Mr. Meno had washed it away.

Yes, that was probably what had happened.

He'd be able to forget about the whole thing.

Beast went down the block and turned the corner.

He stopped at Mr. Meno's driveway.

He didn't see the car. Maybe it was in the garage.

He walked up the driveway.

He stood on tiptoe to look through the garage window.

Even though the window was dusty, he could still see . . . a long scratch across the side of the door.

Beast heard a sound.

Footsteps running.

Then Drake Evans spun him around.

"Stop—" Beast began.

"You stop." Drake let go of him. "Following me around all over the place. And all because of the reward."

Beast took a step back.

Drake looked different . . . not mean, not fresh. Drake looked worried.

Beast shook his head. Why would Drake be worried?

"It wasn't my fault," Drake said. "It was the dog's."

Beast blinked. "What dog?"

"Lester."

"Crazy dog," Beast said.

Drake nodded. "I was just bouncing my ball, and Lester grabbed it."

Beast nodded a little.

"He raced right through Mrs. Alonzo's yard, right through her flowers," Drake said.

Beast sat down on the curb.

He tried to figure out what Drake was telling him.

Drake thought the reward was for him.

Drake thought he was the one who had ruined Mrs. Alonzo's garden.

Beast remembered Emily shaking her head. "How could we have made such a mess?" she had said.

Beast nodded to himself.

Emily was right.

They hadn't made the mess.

Drake had . . . and Lester.

And that was just what Drake was telling him. "I was in the yard just before you were," Drake said.

Beast nodded a little. Drake didn't look mean anymore. He looked worried.

Beast almost felt as if he liked Drake.

"That Lester," said Drake.

Beast nodded. That Lester was trouble.

Chapter 10

It was almost dark. Beast stood on Mr. Meno's front steps.

Mr. Meno had a nice doorbell.

Beast could hear it ringing inside the house. A whole bunch of chimes.

He took a breath.

A moment later Mr. Meno was there, looking down at him.

He had forgotten how tall Mr. Meno was.

He could hardly open his mouth. "The scratch on the door . . ."

Mr. Meno looked surprised. "The front door?"

Beast shook his head. "The side door."

Mr. Meno looked back over his shoulder.

"I shouldn't have been out," Beast said, "but I was trying to get the reward and I ran right into—"

"My side door?" Mr. Meno said. "Up the steps and everything?"

Beast shook his head. "Your car door."

Mr. Meno didn't say anything for a minute. "I wish you had told me that before."

"Yes," Beast said.

"So I wouldn't have blamed Drake Evans . . . so I wouldn't have told him he could never come back here again."

Beast couldn't believe it.

He was really feeling sorry for Drake.

He had felt sorry for Drake all day. Drake helping to water the plants behind Emily's garage. Drake marching right up to Mrs. Alonzo's door and saying he had been the one who wrecked her garden.

And then Beast began to feel a little sorry for himself.

In a loud voice, Mr. Meno was telling him how great his car used to be. That was before every kid in the neighborhood had wrecked it.

Beast nodded. Now he felt sorry for Mr. Meno.

"I'm never going to scratch anyone's car again," Beast said. "And I'm never going to go off the block when I'm not supposed to."

"Never?" Mr. Meno asked. "That's great."

Mr. Meno had opened the door wider. "Want some ice cream?"

"Thanks," Beast said. "But I can't. I'm full."

He had eaten strawberry ice cream at Emily's after lunch . . . and butter pecan at Drake's.

And they all had eaten peach ice cream at Mrs. Alonzo's after they had told her what had happened.

Mrs. Alonzo had turned out to be neat after all.

She was going to help them with Emily's garage garden. "There'll be enough vegetables for everyone," she said.

And tomorrow they were all going to talk with Mrs. Elliot about fencing Lester in.

Beast told Mr. Meno he was sorry one more time. Then he raced back to his own house.

He was going to start another garden. His own garden. Right now. In the dark. Before Holly got the idea.

He couldn't wait to tell her that she and Joanne weren't going to get the reward . . . but he'd never tell her why.

Plant a Garden with the Polk Street School

Contents

77 *Mrs. Alonzo's Tips*

80 *Emily's Salad Garden*

84 *Ms. Rooney's Radishes*

86 *Mrs. Alonzo's Paperwhite Narcissus*

89 *Beast's Vegetable Garden . . . in a Pot*

92 *Holly's Tomatoes*

94 *Drake's Sunflowers*

96 *Joanne's Window Boxes*

99 *Beast's Outdoor Garden*

102 *And Lester Loves Sprouts*

Mrs. Alonzo's Tips:

Everyone should have a garden . . . many gardens.

You can have one or two outdoors. These could be planted in the ground. You could also plant in flowerpots on the back steps, or in window boxes.

You can have gardens indoors too. Put a couple of pots of herbs in the kitchen. Plant a flower or two in a pot on the bathroom windowsill or in your bedroom. You can even have a pot filled with catnip for your favorite cat.

Plants need three things to grow: soil, light, and water.

The soil you use for your garden is important outdoors and indoors. Outdoors, stones and weeds should be taken away. The ground should be raked carefully so that the soil is soft and rainwater can drain into the soil . . . and not lie on top.

When you are planting in pots, make sure each pot has a hole in the bottom. Cover the hole lightly with stones so that water will drain out. Be sure the soil is light and fluffy and not packed down too hard.

Plants need good light too. Indoors, keep your flowerpots near a window or a fluorescent light. Outdoors, plant where your garden will get some sun every day.

Plants need about a half inch of water a day. If it doesn't rain, make sure to give your outdoor plants a gentle drink during the day. You'll have to water your plants indoors when the soil seems dry.

Watch out for large pests like Lester, or tiny insects that leave spots on the leaves. If you do find bugs, take them off the leaves with a small piece of cotton or a Q-tip. Outdoors, be happy when you spot a worm. It digs through the soil, keeping the dirt light and loose. You'll be happy to see ladybugs too. They love to eat aphids, which are pests that live on leaves.

Remember that a florist will often answer your questions and help with your problems. Remember too that you can find library books that tell you about plants and growing them.

Emily's Salad Garden

You can't have a salad without lettuce . . . at least that's what I say. So here's how you do it. You will need:

lettuce seeds
a dishpan
a small bag of pebbles
potting soil
plastic wrap

1. Buy a package of lettuce seeds—leaf lettuce, not the head kind.

2. Find a dishpan and some pebbles.

3. Put an inch of pebbles on the bottom of the dishpan.

4. Fill the dishpan with soil, almost to the top.

5. Gently place the lettuce seeds on top of the soil. Give them room.

6. Sprinkle more soil on top . . . just enough to cover the seeds.

7. Here's the hard part. (Not too hard. Even Beast can do this.) Sprinkle water on top . . . enough water so that each seed is really damp, not enough to drown any of them.

Keep plants away from the radiator.

8. Cover the whole pan with plastic wrap so the seeds don't dry out. Put the pan on a windowsill. Lettuce likes bright light, but not too much sun.

9. Watch as hard as you can. In a couple of days you'll see the first green sprouts. Whip off the plastic wrap.

10. Don't forget to water your lettuce. It likes to stay moist.

11. Invite your friends for salad in about six weeks.

> If you see a plant you like, ask for a cutting. Pop it into a glass of water until you see roots. Then plant.

Ms. Rooney's Radishes

Radishes are almost foolproof. They take only a month to grow, they don't mind a little cold weather, and they look pretty in a salad.

You will need radish seeds and a small patch of ground.

1. Wait for the first spring days, when the frost is off the ground.
2. Make holes in the ground as deep as the tip of your finger and about an inch apart.
3. Drop a seed into each hole.
4. Cover and water gently.

5. Take a look each day. Be sure the soil doesn't dry out. (If you forget to water, the radishes will taste hot!)

6. Watch to see that the radishes are not crowding together. If they are, you may have to pull up a few in between.

7. The radishes are ready when you see their red tops poking out of the ground.

> Plant marigolds near vegetables. They keep the bugs away.

Mrs. Alonzo's Paperwhite Narcissus

Are you sick of winter? Rush down to the florist for a paperwhite narcissus bulb. It won't look like much when you first see it. You may think you're buying an onion!

You'll be surprised, though. It doesn't take long for the bulb to sprout. It will send out tall green stems and a cluster of beautiful white flowers.

You'll need:

a cup or an empty eight-ounce milk container

a fistful of pebbles
a paperwhite narcissus bulb

> Indoor plants like the temperature to be 60 to 70 degrees.

It's important to ask the florist if the bulb will need cold and darkness first. If the florist says yes, be sure to add in step 4 below. If the florist says no, skip step 4.

Here's how it works:

1. Put about an inch of pebbles in the bottom of the cup.

2. Gently place the narcissus bulb on top of the pebbles. Add enough pebbles to cover up to the bulb shoulders. The top must be sticking out.

3. Add water just to the bottom of the bulb.

4. If your florist tells you this paperwhite needs darkness, put the bulb in its cup in a cool dark place for about ten days. The basement is fine. Then bring it up-stairs.

5. Keep watching your bulb. You may need to add water once in a while.

Your bulb will grow fast. Every day you'll see a difference. The flowers usually appear within two weeks.

You can plant other bulbs too. Ask the man in the flower store.

Beast's Vegetable Garden . . . in a Pot

Gather together a bunch of flowerpots. It's a lot easier than raking and pulling a million weeds. Make sure each pot has a hole in the bottom so that water will drain out. Put a couple of small stones on top of each hole. Then fill each pot with potting soil. Find a nice sunny spot on the patio.

For carrots you will need:

carrot seeds that say "tiny" or "short"
a pot that's five inches across and six inches deep

Plant about as deep as the tip of your pinky. You'll have a carrot before the end of the summer.

For beets you will need:

beet seeds
a pot that is at least seven inches
across and seven inches deep

Plant a few seeds about an inch apart. When they start to grow, pull out all but one. If you plant when school is over, you'll have a beet by the end of the summer.

Water!
Wait!
Weed!

Holly's Tomatoes

You will need:

a tomato plant or seeds
a pot at least ten inches deep and twelve inches across—the bigger the better!
potting soil
a few pebbles for drainage
a sturdy stick
a twist-tie

When your tomato plant is five or six inches tall, make a crutch for it by standing the stick up in the pot and tying it to the plant with the twist-tie. This will make the plant grow tall and straight.

Plant an apple seed you've dug out of an apple . . .

A grapefruit seed from your breakfast grapefruit . . .

A lemon seed . . .

No fruit, but great plants.

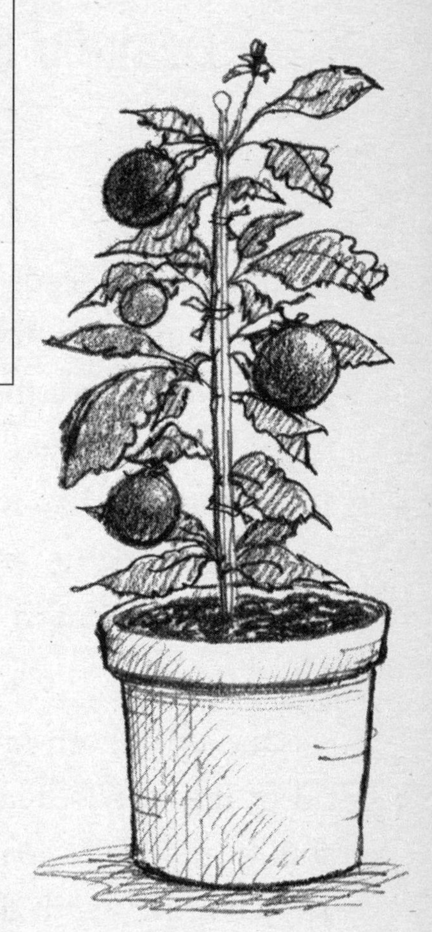

Drake's Sunflowers

You will need:

sunflower seeds . . . or save some from the box you were eating. (Make sure they haven't been roasted. Make sure they still have their shells on.) The seeds are big and easy to work with.

a sunny spot in the garden

Rake up the ground so that it's soft. Get rid of the weeds. Plant the sunflower seeds about an inch apart. Then stand back. They'll grow *fast*. If they seem crowded, pull out a few. Water every few days, or when they look a little limp.

These are interesting plants to watch. Each day they turn their flower heads to follow the sun. By the end of the summer they may be as tall as a full-grown man. You'll see that their heads are full of seeds. The birds will love them!

Joanne's Window Boxes

Window boxes are fun, but they can be heavy. Ask for help to be sure they are attached firmly to your windowsill. Or leave them on the back step. You can fill a win-

dow box with a few herb plants and mix in a flower or two. Just make sure you choose plants that won't grow too tall.

Herbs like chives and parsley are fun. Snip off a small bunch. Wash and add to your sandwich!

You will need:

a window box (Make sure there are holes in the bottom for water to drain through.)
pebbles
potting soil

1. Place a layer of pebbles on the bottom of the window box. Add soil.
2. Water gently so the soil is moist.
3. Add seeds or small plants.

Try a peppermint plant.

Suggestions:

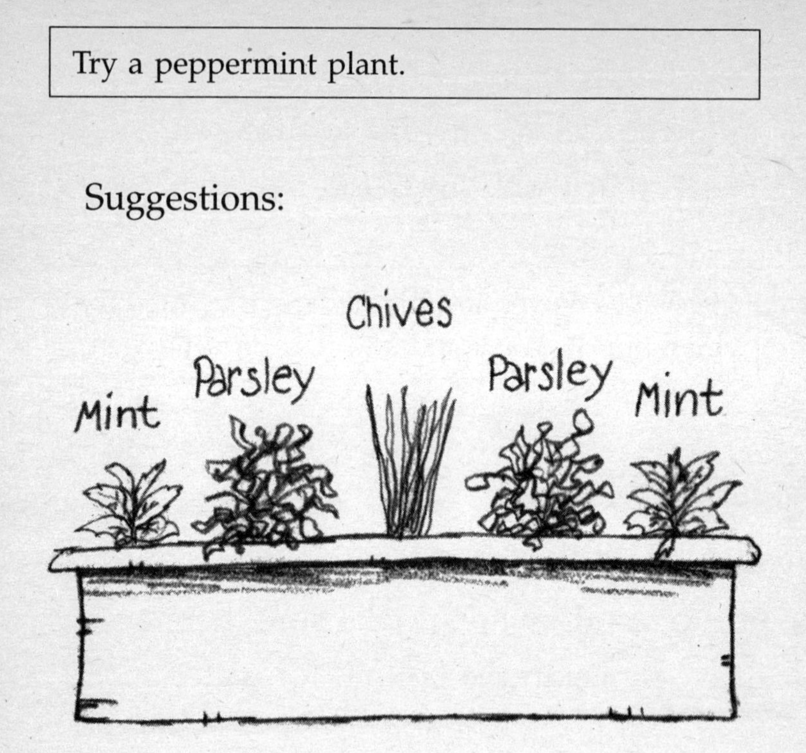

Beast's Outdoor Garden

Start with a small patch. It can be as long as you are tall and as wide as your arms. You'll have to rake, and throw away stones, and make sure the soil is fluffy. It's hard work.

You'll have to weed too.

You will need:

- a rake
- a watering can
- a small ball of twine and wooden or plastic stakes to keep out pests like Lester

Here's a suggestion for a red-white-and-blue garden:

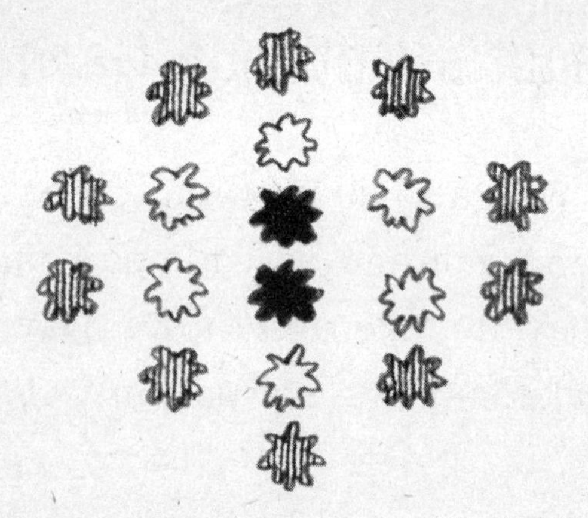

Hummingbirds love red! Put lots of red flowers in your garden.

1. Plant two red petunias in the middle.

2. Plant six white alyssum around the petunias.

3. Plant ten blue ageratum around the alyssum.

4. You can surround the entire garden with stones or shells.

And Lester Loves Sprouts

This is really growing seeds for your salad in water. There are a couple of ways to do it.

For the first way you will need:

a clean sponge
water
a saucer
mustard seeds or alfalfa seeds from
the health-food store

1. Run water over the sponge to moisten it. Place the sponge on the saucer.
2. Scatter the seeds on top.
3. Put the saucer in a sunny window.

4. Check regularly to be sure the sponge is still damp. You may need to add water.

Your salad greens will be ready in a few days.

For the second way you will need:

mustard seeds or alfalfa seeds
a clean jar
a piece of cheesecloth or screen to cover the top
water

1. Put the seeds in the bottom of the jar. Cover them with water and leave them overnight.

2. The next morning, empty the water.

3. Put the jar in a dim place.

4. In the afternoon, empty the water again.

5. Do this twice a day.

6. When the seeds are almost as big as your thumb, put them in a sunny spot.

They'll be ready to eat in a few more days.